KV-061-990

THE ADVENTURES OF DEVONTAY AND PINEAPPLE

by Fenyang Smith & Summerlynn Burlew

©2021 Devontay and Pineapple all rights reserved.
Written by Fenyang Smith
Illustrated by Summerlynn Burlew
ISBN: 978-1-7363233-0-4

For ordering information & to learn more,
reach out to us at:

IG: @devontayandpineapple
Email: devontayandpineapple@gmail.com

To our early readers, and all the talented young artists who shared their creative genius and imaginative perspectives with us.

To Devontae and Taylor whose spirits of wonder, curiosity, and love brought so much life to these pages and to our hearts.

To all those who believe in magic, adventure, and dreams.
We dedicate this book to you.
With all our gratitude and love,

—Yani & Sum

Devontay didn't want to spend his summer vacation out in the countryside.

As he walked up the dusty path to his Grandma's house, his face looked as gloomy as the gray sky above.

"What's wrong, Devontay?" Grandma asked him with a kind smile.

"I don't like it here," Devontay grumbled. "I want to go back home to the city,"

"I know it may not look like it, but there is more to this place than meets the eye," Grandma told him.

"The most beautiful things are sometimes hidden right around us."

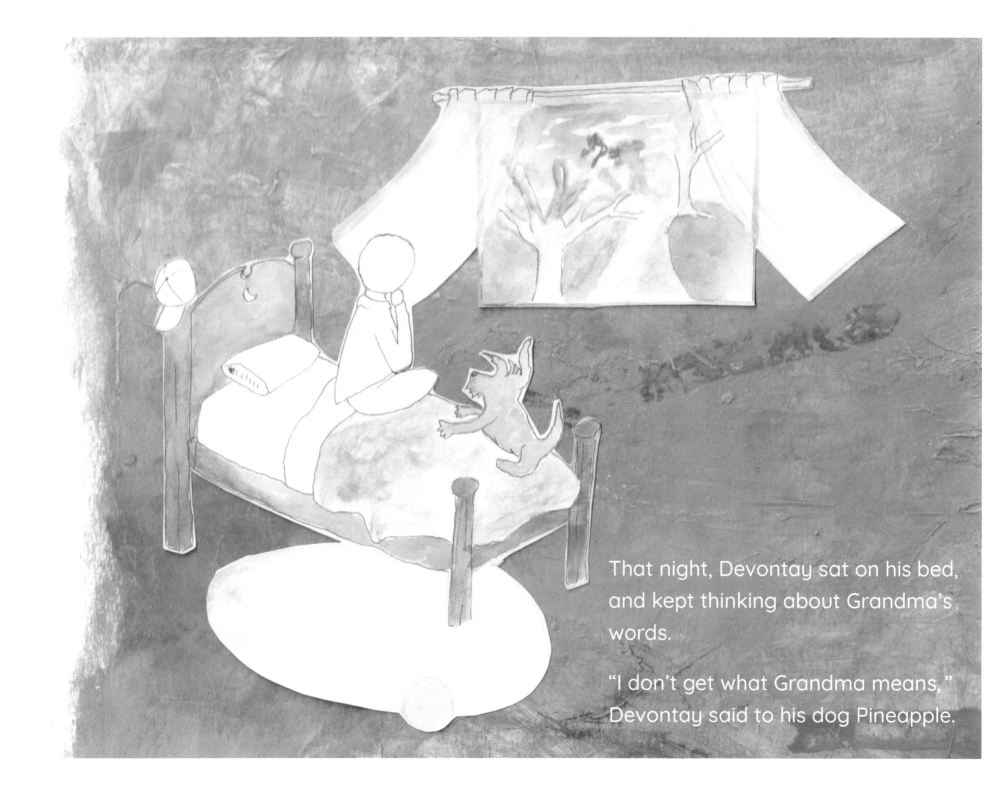

That night, Devontay sat on his bed, and kept thinking about Grandma's words.

"I don't get what Grandma means," Devontay said to his dog Pineapple.

Just as he was about to lay down, a pale-blue light stretched right across his blanket.

Devontay saw the fluffy, white clouds open up like curtains, revealing a bright full moon.

"Wow!" Devontay exclaimed, "I've never seen the sky look so big!"

Devontay jumped to the window and peeked outside. In the moonlight, he saw a glittering bunch of what looked like rubies. "Is that treasure?" he asked.

Pineapple woofed excitedly.
"Maybe there is something cool out here, huh boy?"
Devontay said, grinning at Pineapple.

The next morning, Devontay and Pineapple woke up super early...

eager to discover what the moon had shown them.

"Where are you two headed in such a rush?"
Grandma asked.

"On an adventure!"
Devontay said with a bright smile.

"How wonderful!" Grandma replied.

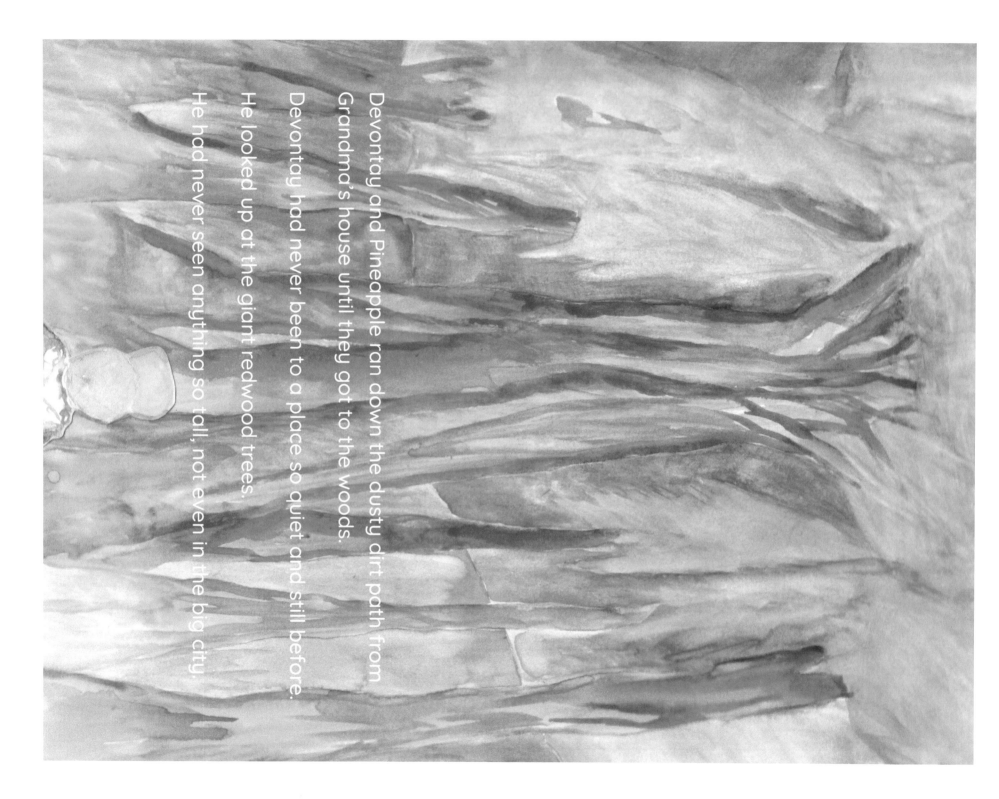

Devontay and Pineapple ran down the dusty dirt path from Grandma's house until they got to the woods.

Devontay had never been to a place so quiet and still before.

He looked up at the giant redwood trees.

He had never seen anything so tall, not even in the big city.

They kept walking, and soon began to hear strange noises.
Before long, they came upon a small pond where
a group of frogs were hopping and singing together.

They looked down into the pond and saw lots of colorful fish.

"It's not so lonely here," Devontay said to Pineapple.

"There's all kinds of creatures here with us."

Suddenly, they heard a sound like a humongous frog.
But it wasn't a frog!

It was just Devontay's tummy mumbling and grumbling.

"I guess it's time for lunch, huh Pineapple?"
Devontay laughed and they ran all the way back to
Grandma's house.

That night, Devontay and Pineapple looked excitedly out of their bedroom window.

"I wonder what we'll find tomorrow,"
Devontay asked thoughtfully.

The next morning, while Grandma cooked breakfast, Devontay drew a picture of a frog band and an audience of fishes.

"I love the music of those frogs!" Grandma said.

Grandma rested a warm hand on Devontay's shoulder and looked him in the eyes.

"You're quite an amazing artist, Devontay," she said kindly.

"I can't wait to hear about your adventures today!"

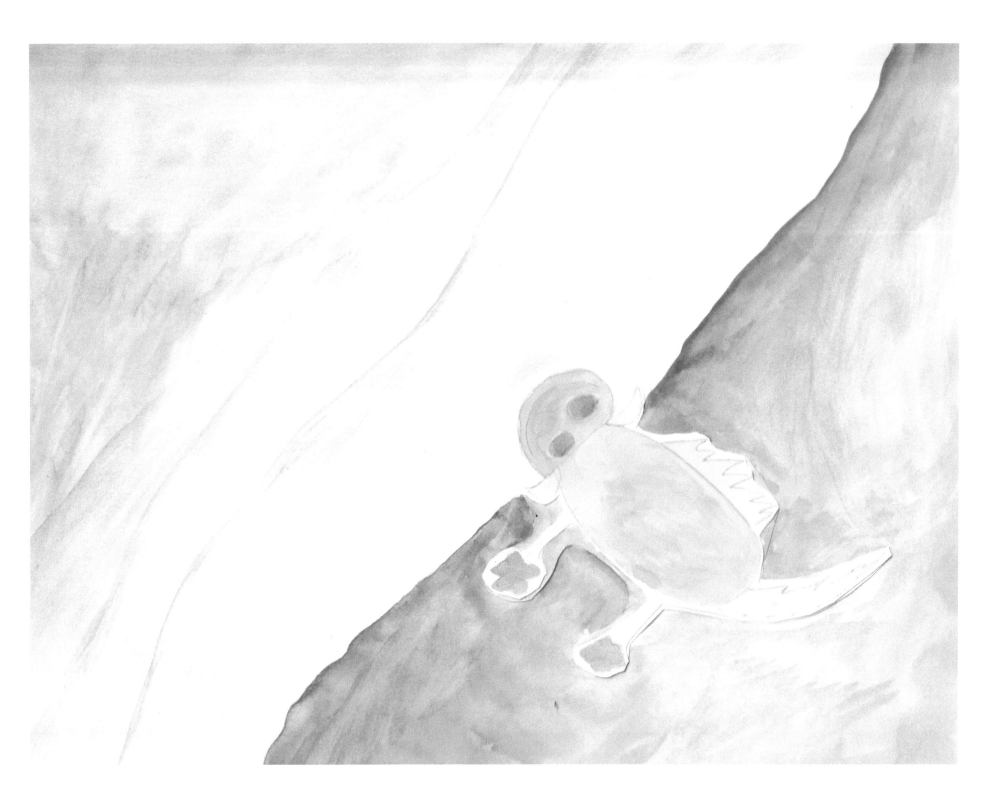

Devontay and Pineapple
spent the afternoon skipping
stones by the pond.

It was starting to get late,
and even though the sun
had already begun to set,
Devontay was determined to
skip just one more stone.

"Watch this!" Devontay said.

Devontay pulled back...and let it fly!
The stone jumped, and jumped...

And jumped, and jumped...

...And landed in a big bush that glittered with bright, red **rubies.**

"Look Pineapple, treasure!" Devontay shouted.

They were starting to walk towards the bush when...

Devontay and Pineapple ran, and ran, and ran...

...all the way back to their room and hopped right under the covers.

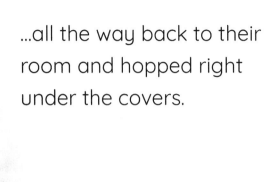
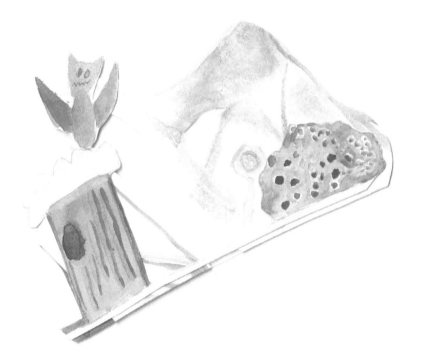

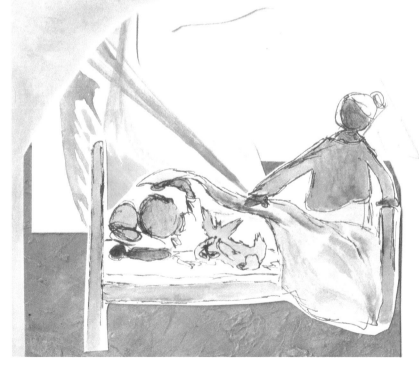

Before long, Grandma came to see what all the trouble was.

"What's wrong, Devontay?" she asked.

"We s-saw a m—m-monster!!" he stuttered.

"Really?" asked Grandma. "What kind of monster?"

Devontay tried to show her:
"It had **big horns, sharp claws,
and HUGE eyes!**"

"That sounds pretty scary!" Grandma said.
"You and Pineapple must have been very brave."

Devontay also told Grandma about the bush that shined bright with rubies.

"It sounds like you found some treasure! Will you bring me some tomorrow?" Grandma asked.

"But what about the monster?" Devontay asked worriedly.

"Don't worry," Grandma said. "I think you'll find he's not so scary in the morning."

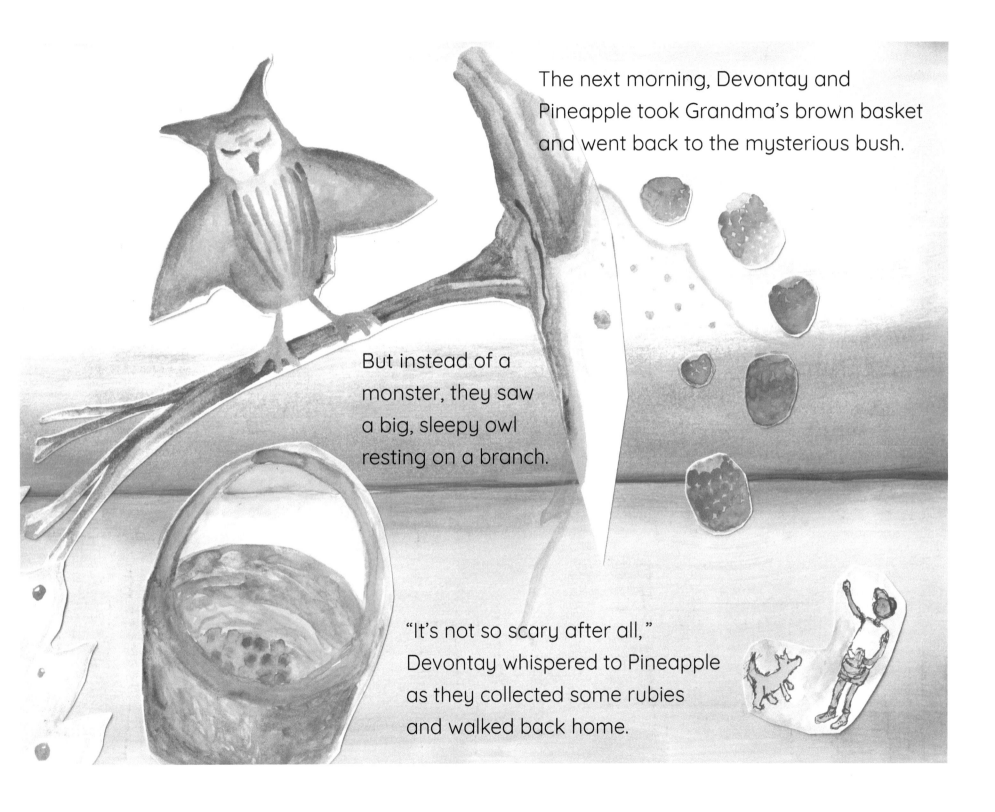

The next morning, Devontay and Pineapple took Grandma's brown basket and went back to the mysterious bush.

But instead of a monster, they saw a big, sleepy owl resting on a branch.

"It's not so scary after all," Devontay whispered to Pineapple as they collected some rubies and walked back home.

"Did you see the monster?"
Grandma asked as she placed a big bowl of rubies
on the table.

"No, Grandma,"
Devontay
laughed.
"It was
AMAZING!
It was a great,
big owl."

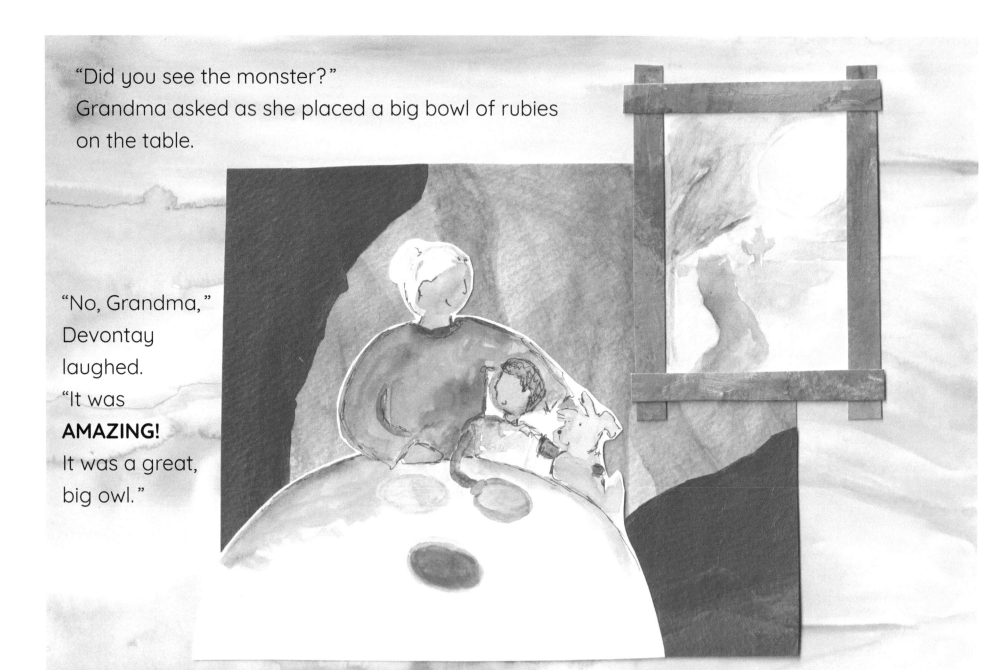

"Sometimes things are less scary when we can see them clearly," Grandma said.
"I hope it's not too scary being here in a new place."

"I'm not scared."
Devontay said.
"In fact…"

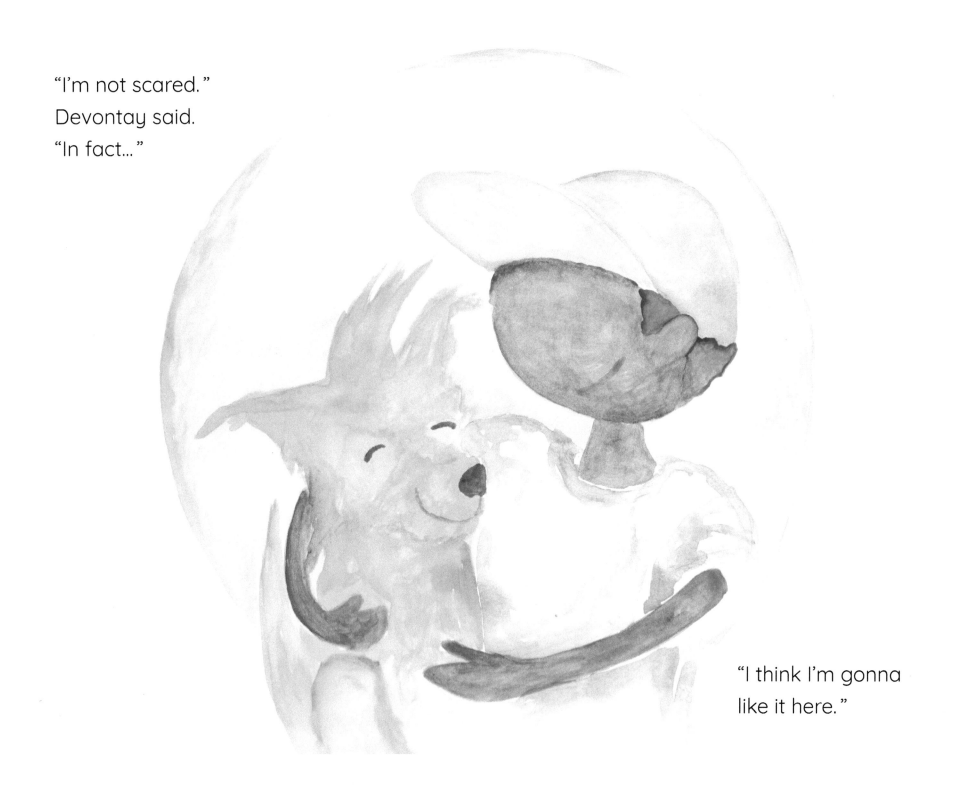

"I think I'm gonna
like it here."

CPSIA information can be obtained
at www.ICGtesting.com
Printed in the USA
BVHW090402130321
602042BV00001B/1